HarperPerennial
A Division of HarperCollins*Publishers*

W9-ATL-706

Dogs Are Worth It!

PEANUTS TREASURY

Charles M. Schulz

HarperCollins books may be purchased for
educational, business, or sales promotional use.
For information please write to:
Special Markets Department, HarperCollins Publishers, Inc.,
10 East 53rd Street, New York, NY 10022

http://www.harpercollins.com

Designed by Christina Bliss, Staten Island

ISBN 0-06-107563-9

Printed in U.S.A.

3

6

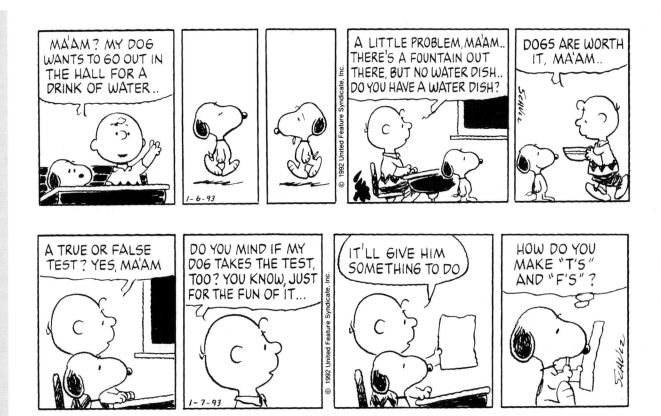

7

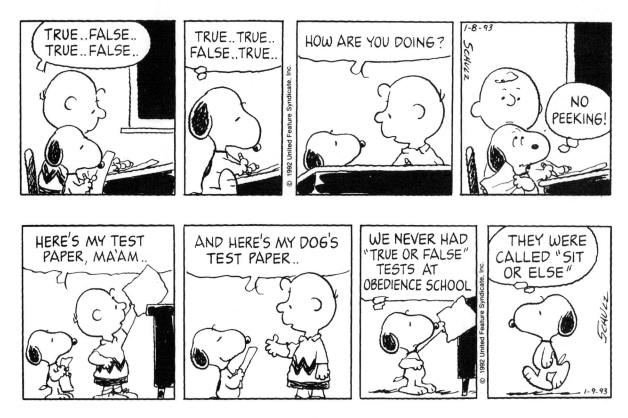

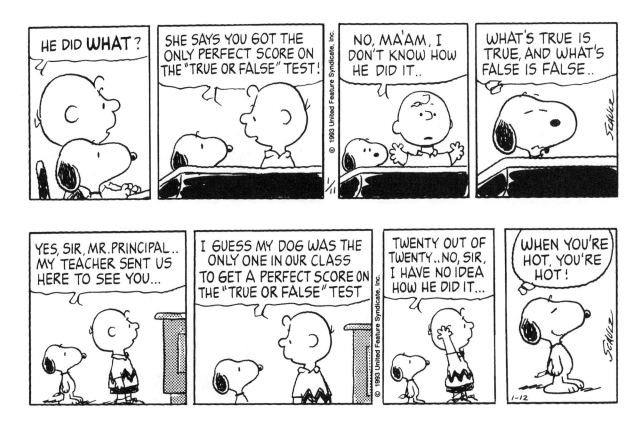

9

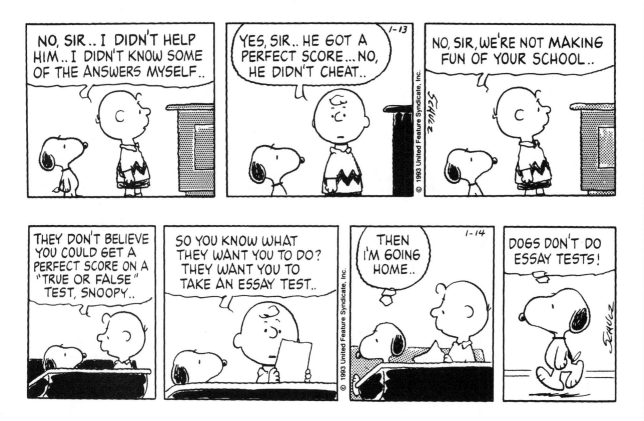

11

13

15

16

17

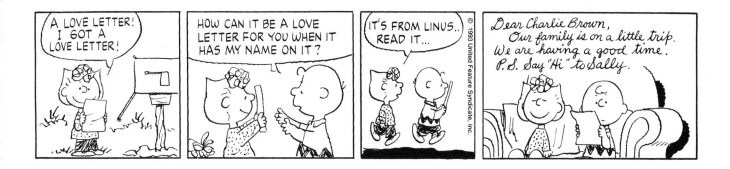

21

22

23

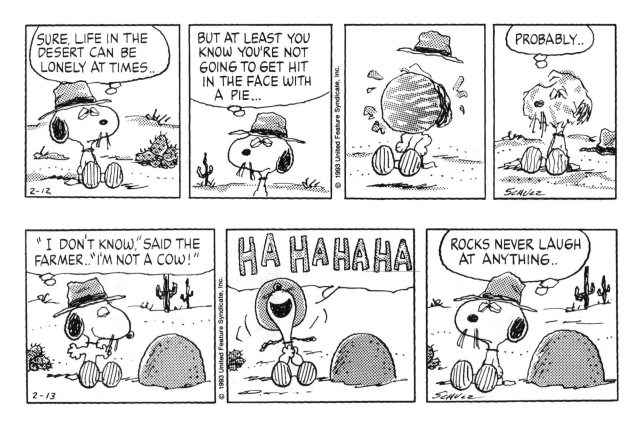

24

25

ROCK SLIDE AREA

26

31

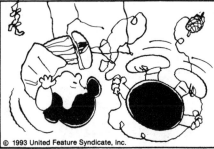

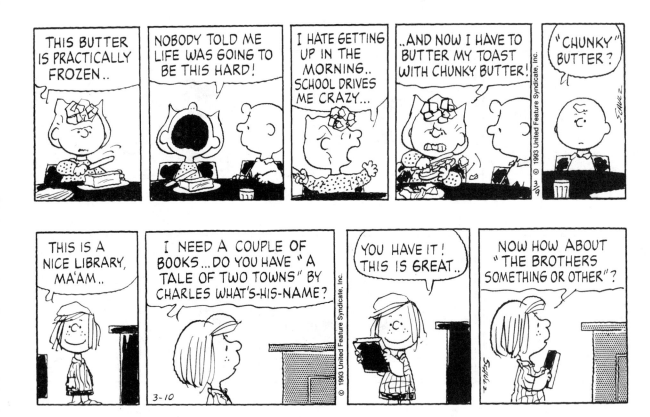

36

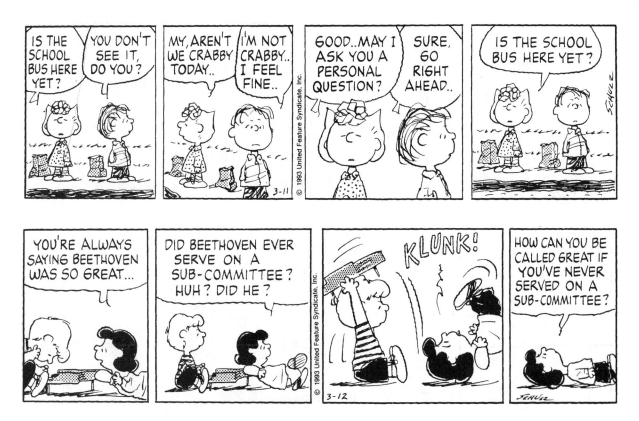

37

39

40

41

42

43

44

45

46

55

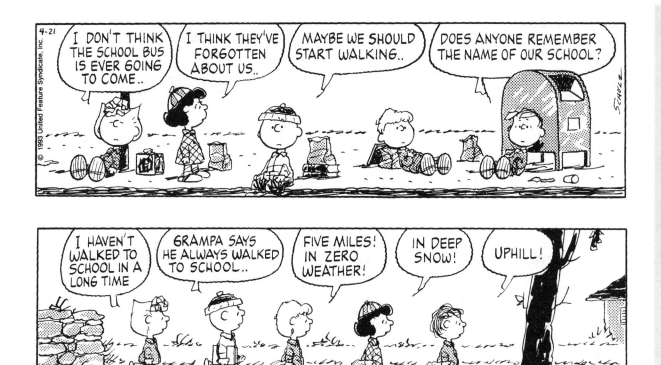

58

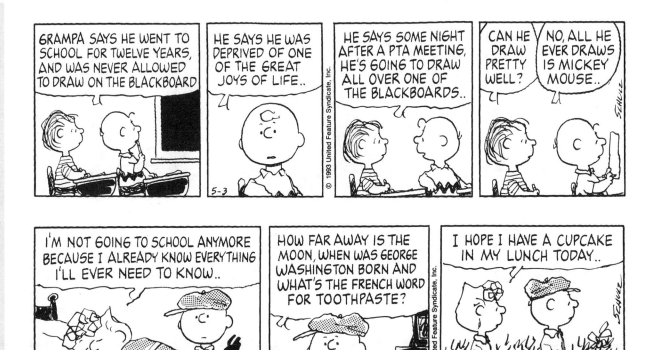

63

64

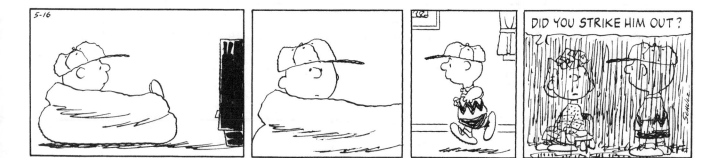

70

74

75

77

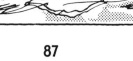

88

93

94

95

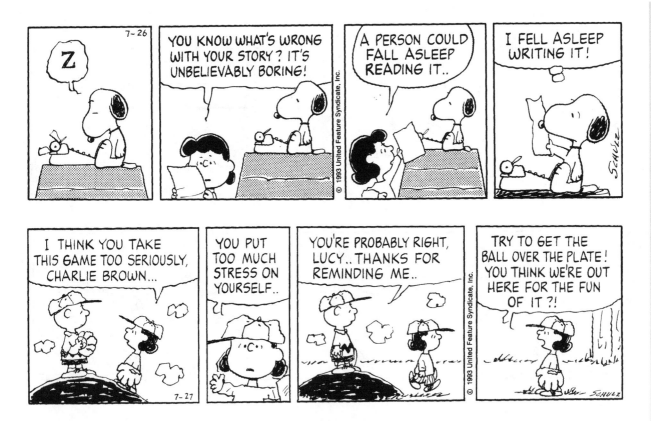

102

104

105

107

113

115

116

119

123

125

126

127

130

132

133

134

135

136

139

141

142

143

144

149

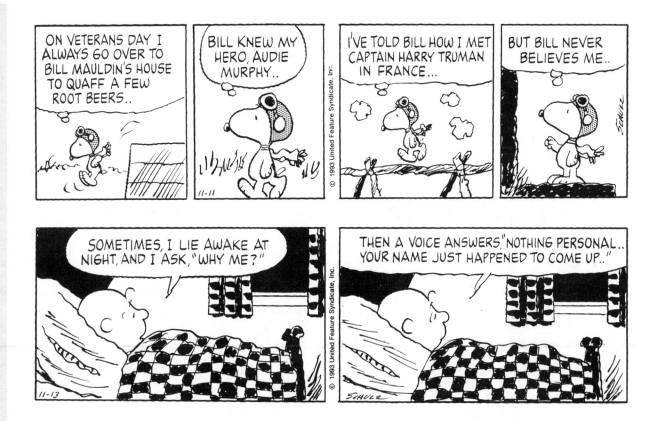

153

158

159

160

161

164

165

166

167

169

170

171

172

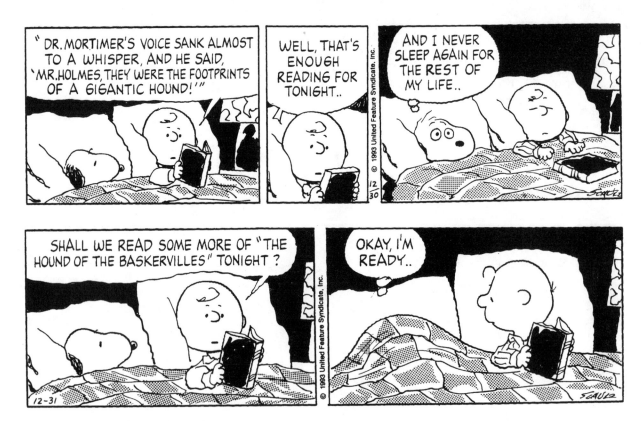